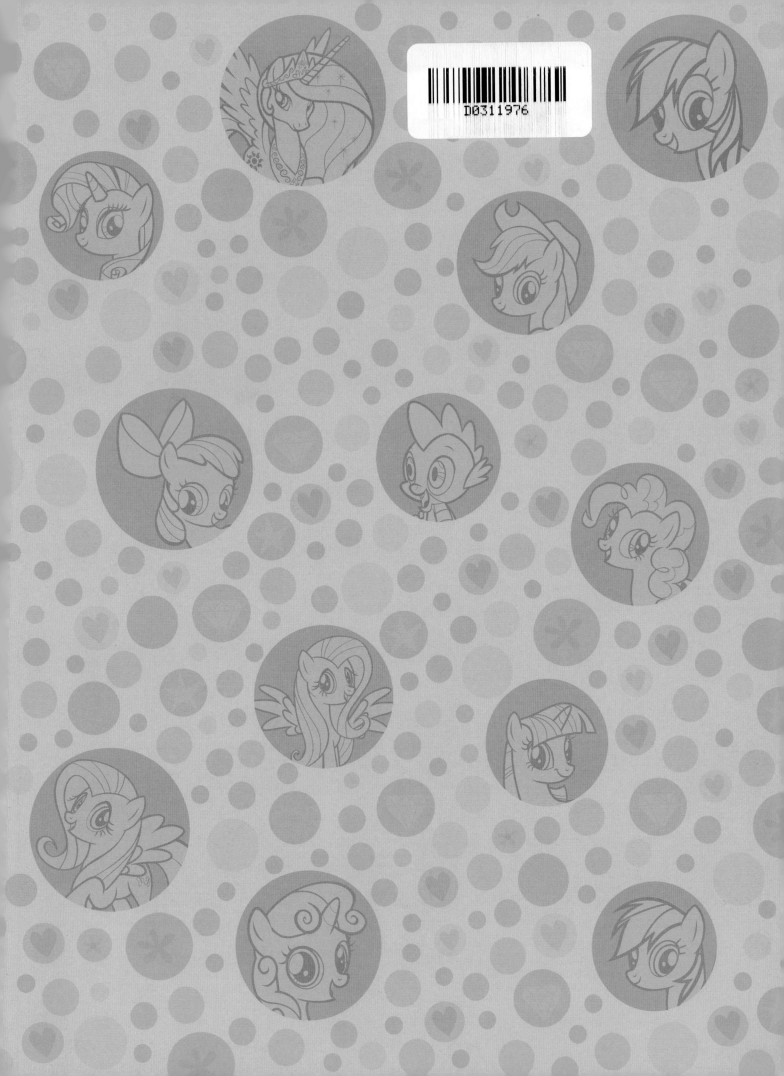

This book belongs to

♡...Mabel Jean♡Holder...x x

♡♡♡♡♡ ♡ ♡ / ♡
....

ORCHARD BOOKS
Carmelite House
50 Victoria Embankment
London EC4Y 0DZ

First published in 2015 by Orchard Books

ISBN 978 1 40833 692 2

A CIP catalogue record for this book is available from the British Library.

1 3 5 7 9 10 8 6 4 2

Printed in China

Orchard Books is an imprint of Hachette Children's Group
Part of The Watts Publishing Group Limited, an Hachette UK company.

www.hachette.co.uk

Adult supervision is recommended for all baking
and cooking activities, and when
glue, paint, scissors and other
sharp points are in use.

My Little Pony

Annual 2016

ORCHARD

Contents

Welcome!

Hello pony friend,

Welcome to our new super-fun annual!

We just love games, stories and activities, and we know you'll enjoy all of the special treats inside this book. Try some of Pinkie Pie's delicious recipes, discover your perfect pet with Fluttershy, and even star in your very own My Little Pony adventure! There's lots of top-secret info about your favourite funny fillies, the Cutie Mark Crusaders, and much, much more. Come and join in the fun!

With love,

Your My Little Pony friends

x x x x x x

IMPORTANT INTROS

These six pony pals are always at the heart of the action!

TWILIGHT SPARKLE

Princess Celestia sent Twilight Sparkle to Ponyville to learn all about friendship. She proved herself to be a true friend by bringing together five special ponies and destroying Nightmare Moon!

RAINBOW DASH

Loyal Rainbow Dash is a true adventurer! She speeds across the skies of Equestria, helping the sun to shine and guiding storm clouds wherever they are needed.

PINKIE PIE

Pinkie Pie brings fun and laughter to everything she does. This chatty little pony loves nothing more than a giggly, gossipy get-together, and is always on hoof to plan a party!

RARITY

Elegant Rarity is the most fashionable pony in all of Equestria! She makes amazing outfits in her stylish boutique. She knows that true beauty is on the inside, and this generous pony would do anything for her friends.

FLUTTERSHY

As well as her pony pals, kind Fluttershy has lots of animal friends. This quiet pony is happiest in her peaceful cottage in the middle of the forest. Although she has wings, Fluttershy would rather keep her hooves on the ground!

APPLEJACK

Energetic Applejack can usually be found out and about in Sweet Apple Acres! Her honesty and loyalty make her a truly fantastic friend.

Awesome Apple Bloom

Apple Bloom is the leader of the Cutie Mark Crusaders!

Superstar sister: Apple Bloom is Applejack's younger sister.

Cutie Mark Crusaders: Apple Bloom leads this group of young ponies. The crusaders want their cutie marks more than anything . . . but in their search for their destiny, they sometimes end up finding trouble!

Home: Sweet Apple Acres with Applejack, Granny Smith, Big Mac and the rest of the family!

Down to Earth: Apple Bloom is an Earth Pony. Earth Ponies don't have wings or a unicorn horn, and they help to look after the land of Equestria.

Pony personality: Apple Bloom is brave and loyal. She is also a *teensy tiny bit* clumsy!

Missing marks:

The Cutie Mark Crusaders are desperate to get their cutie marks! The older ponies tell them that their unique talents will be revealed in good time, but the young crusaders are very impatient . . .

Spot the Difference

Can you spot the five differences in these two pictures of the Cutie Mark Crusaders?

Turn to page 62 for the answers.

5

11

Magical Mystery Cure

It was a beautiful day in Ponyville. Twilight Sparkle sang a happy song as she trotted into town.

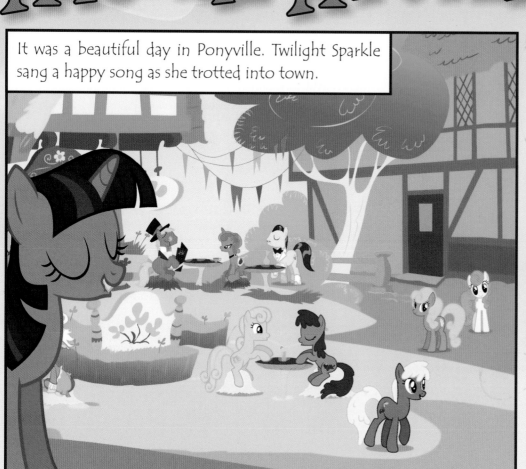

Suddenly, a large raincloud appeared and soaked Twilight Sparkle. "Rainbow Dash, that is NOT funny!" she cried. But then she saw *Rarity* was trying to control the weather!

All of Twilight Sparkle's friends had the wrong cutie marks! Poor Fluttershy was struggling to be as funny as Pinkie Pie, Applejack was having a dress disaster and Pinkie Pie was making a terrible mess down at Sweet Apple Acres.

Oh no! Twilight Sparkle realised that *she* had caused the cutie mark chaos. Princess Celestia had asked for her help with a special spell, and Twilight Sparkle had read it aloud. The spell had mixed up the cutie marks!

Twilight Sparkle saw that Rarity had Rainbow Dash's cutie mark on her flank! "Rarity, what happened to *your* cutie mark?" she asked. But Rarity insisted that the cutie mark was hers!

Rarity and Twilight Sparkle headed to Fluttershy's cottage, but Rainbow Dash opened the door. Inside, Fluttershy's animal friends were causing a terrible mess!

"Their true selves have been altered!" wept Twilight Sparkle. "And I don't have a cure! I have to find a way to make this right . . . "

Twilight Sparkle realised that the only way to fix things was to make sure her friends helped each other. That way, they would remember their true destinies.

Rainbow Dash was in BIG trouble with the angry animals! But kind Fluttershy made everyone feel better. As Fluttershy hugged her animal pals, a magical glow surrounded her and the right cutie mark appeared on her side!

Next, Rainbow Dash helped Rarity with the weather, and *her* cutie mark was returned! Together, the pony pals worked to help all of their friends return to normal.

"You look just like a princess!" breathed Fluttershy.
"That's because she *is* a princess!" said a soft voice. It was Princess Celestia!

"A p-p-princess?!" stammered Twilight Sparkle. Princess Celestia nodded. "You are an inspiration to us all, Twilight," she said gravely, bowing down before the stunned pony.

Twilight Sparkle suddenly realised that she knew how to complete the spell. But as she completed it, she was magically transported to a mysterious place, full of stars. Princess Celestia appeared next to her.

"It's time for you to fulfil *your* destiny," said wise Princess Celestia. In a huge flash of light, Twilight Sparkle found herself back in Ponyville. As her friends surrounded her, they saw that Twilight Sparkle had wings!

The next day, an amazing ceremony was held at Canterlot Castle, and Princess Twilight Sparkle was officially crowned!

Princess Twilight Sparkle knew that her special friendships had helped her to become a princess. She felt like the luckiest pony in the whole of Equestria!

Princess in Training

Twilight Sparkle couldn't believe it when Princess Celestia made her a princess! The studious pony was determined to become the perfect princess. But how? Luckily, Twilight Sparkle's friends had lots of advice and tips for her.

"Is there a book about being a princess that I should read?!"

"A princess needs to look good and feel confident. You can count on me to make you wonderful outfits that will help you feel like radiant royalty from mane to hoof!"

"Whoopee! This calls for a princess party, party, party! I'm going to make a special strawberry sundae . . . AND a GIANT cupcake shaped like a crown . . . AND a trifle topped with sprinkles. We're going to celebrate Pinkie Pie style!"

"I can't believe I'm a companion to a *real* princess! Hmm . . . does this mean I can eat delicious gems for every meal?!"

"A true princess is hard-working and ain't afraid to get her hooves dirty! You'll always be welcome to applebuck with us down at the farm."

"Congratulations, Princess T! *I'm* the one to teach you how to use those new wings. You need to be whizzy if you want to rule the sky!"

"Don't worry, Twilight Sparkle! I made you a princess as you've shown compassion, devotion, integrity and leadership. You're a natural princess!"

17

All About You!

You already know lots about your pony friends, and now they want to learn all about you!

My name is Mabel Hoder **Age** 7

This is me
Draw a picture of yourself

My birthday is

5th of sob

My family
Draw a picture of your family

My favourite things

Colour ...... purple ....

Toy ...... lots ....

Animal ...... owl + elagant ....

My Little Pony ...... Fluter Shi ....

Book ...... wirst wich ....

Food ...... backd botato ....

My best friend

Draw a picture
of your best friend

My hobbies

....

....

....

....

TOO MANY PINKIE PIES

When Pinkie Pie discovered a magical mirror pool, she created *lots* of Pinkie Pie clones! Can you count how many there are in the picture below? Write the total at the bottom of the page.

Turn to page 62 for the answer.

ANSWER

20

Beautiful Boutique

Rarity is about to start work on next season's designs, but the Carousel Boutique is completely empty! Use your pens, pencils and stickers to add mirrors and clothes rails. Can you draw some stylish clothes and accessories, too?

SUPER SCOOTALOO

Scootaloo is a member of the Cutie Mark Crusaders!

Speedy scooting: This little pony loves to whizz around Ponyville on her scooter at top speed!

Pony personality: Scootaloo is full of energy and is a bit of a tomboy. She hates brushing her mane and tail, and her hair often sticks up!

Flying hero! Scootaloo *loves* Rainbow Dash and thinks she is the coolest pony in Ponyville! Rainbow Dash often takes the little pony under her wing and gives her advice.

Training wings: Scootaloo is a Pegasus Pony, so she has little wings, but she hasn't yet learned to fly properly. For now, she's happy on her scooter!

Mystery marks: Just like her friends Apple Bloom and Sweetie Belle, Scootaloo is desperate for her cutie mark to appear!

SCOOTALOO'S SPEEDY WORD SEARCH

Can you find the six words connected to Scootaloo and her fellow Cutie Mark Crusaders hidden in the grid?

Turn to page 62 for the answers.

```
D  C  L  U  B  H  O  U  S  E
E  E  I  O  T  C  L  L  Y  A
S  K  N  P  W  U  T  I  W  D
T  A  L  E  N  T  O  N  X  V
I  G  Y  Y  Z  I  W  L  U  E
N  V  L  Z  L  E  S  K  R  N
Y  J  W  Q  W  M  N  Y  S  T
M  L  P  E  G  A  S  U  S  U
U  E  S  I  H  R  W  R  H  R
S  I  P  Q  E  K  L  N  K  E
```

Cutie Mark   Adventure

Destiny   Pegasus

Talent   Clubhouse

23

Pinkie Pie's Princess Party

When Twilight Sparkle became a princess, Pinkie Pie threw her a super-fun party! Here are two of the tasty treats she served. Don't forget to ask a grown-up to help you with these recipes.

Fantastic Fruity Punch

Ingredients

★ Two handfuls of fruit, such as strawberries, raspberries and an orange

★ One lime

★ One carton of pineapple juice

★ One bottle of sparkling water

★ Ice

★ A large jug

1 Ask a grown-up to chop the fruit into bite-size pieces and cut the lime in half.

2 Put lots of ice in the bottom of a jug and then add half a carton of pineapple juice. Top up with sparkling water and stir.

3 Add the fruit to the top of the drink and squeeze lime juice over the top.

4 Serve right away!

Chocolicious Cookies

Ingredients

★ 150g butter, softened
★ 60g light brown muscovado sugar
★ 60g granulated sugar
★ 2 tsp vanilla extract
★ 1 large egg, beaten
★ 225g plain flour
★ ½ tsp bicarbonate of soda
★ ¼ tsp salt
★ 200g plain chocolate chips or chunks

This recipe makes around thirty cookies.

① Ask a grown-up to preheat the oven to 190C/170C fan/ gas mark 5. Line two baking trays with baking paper.

② Put the butter and two types of sugar into a bowl, and beat until creamy. Add in the vanilla extract and beaten egg.

③ Next, sieve the flour, bicarbonate of soda and salt into the mixture and mix in with a wooden spoon. Add the chocolate chips and stir well.

④ Using a teaspoon, place small mounds of the mixture on the baking trays. Keep the mounds a good distance apart as the mixture will spread out when it's cooking!

⑤ Ask a grown-up to put the trays in the oven and bake the cookies for 8–10 minutes until light brown on the edges and still slightly soft in the centre.

⑥ Leave on the tray for a couple of minutes to firm up and then transfer to a cooling rack.

Pinkie Pie's top tip:
These cookies are just as delicious if you replace the chocolate chips with raisins!

Missing Marks

Oh no! The ponies have lost their cutie marks! Can you help reunite each pony with their special mark?

Turn to page 62 for the answers.

Race to the Wonderbolts

The Wonderbolts have asked Rainbow Dash to take a supersonic flight with them, but first the fast filly has to make it through the maze. Can you help her?

Turn to page 62 for the answer.

The Show Stoppers

Applejack led the three Cutie Mark Crusaders through a forest on the edge of Sweet Apple Acres. Suddenly, she stopped in front of a rundown tree house.

"Cutie Mark Crusaders, welcome to your new clubhouse!" she cried.

In no time at all, Apple Bloom had fixed up the clubhouse. The three young fillies now had a base where they could plan how to get their cutie marks! The crusaders wanted their cutie marks more than anything else in the world.

In the clubhouse, Sweetie Belle made up a new theme song for the crusaders, and Scootaloo drew a map of Ponyville. They were ready to discover their unique talents and get their cutie marks!

"We'll leave no stone unturned!" cried Apple Bloom.

"We'll leave no mountain unclimbed!" shouted Scootaloo.

"And no dinner uncooked," chimed in Sweetie Belle. "Let's go!"

The young friends headed out into Ponyville to lend a hoof to whoever needed it. They felt sure that this would help them discover where their talent and destiny lay! But, after helping out at the farm, the sweet shop and the boutique, all they'd done was make a mess – and there was *still* no sign of their marks.

The ponies headed to the Golden Oak Library to see if there was a book that could help them.

Kind Twilight Sparkle gave the ponies a flyer for a talent show.

"You need to think about what you're *already* good at," she advised.

Later that day, the three friends travelled around Ponyville, pulled by Scootaloo on her super-speedy scooter. They gathered together all kinds of objects: Rarity's dress designs, planks of wood, cans of paint . . . and even a book on ghouls and goblins!

"What *are* they up to?" wondered Twilight Sparkle.

The three crusaders had decided to put on a dramatic piece for the talent show, with a super-cool song, amazing costumes and mind-blowing dance moves!

"This is going to be SO awesome!" cried Scootaloo.

The friends decided what their roles would be. Even though Sweetie Belle was a wonderful singer, she decided she would design the costumes and scenery. Scootaloo couldn't really sing, but she wanted to perform a rock ballad! And Apple Bloom decided to show off her favourite kung fu moves.

"Let's get started!" smiled Sweetie Belle.

But the rehearsals didn't go well. The young ponies struggled to get it right, even though they all helped each other as much as possible.

Applejack popped by the clubhouse and saw what was going on. She knew their performance would be a disaster!

It was time for the talent show, and the whole of Ponyville was in the audience! The three Cutie Mark Crusaders waited nervously backstage. Twilight Sparkle wished them the very best of luck.

As Scootaloo started to sing her song about the Cutie Mark Crusaders, the crowd fell silent. She couldn't sing at all! Sweetie Belle's scenery began to fall apart, and Apple Bloom kept falling over as she did her kung fu moves.

When the ponies finished their performance, the audience started to *laugh*! The crusaders couldn't believe it when they won the award for best comedy act! They hadn't meant their performance to be funny.

"I *knew* our performance was awesome!" shouted Scootaloo.

"I wonder if we've got our cutie marks," said Apple Bloom excitedly, but when they took off their costumes, the three friends were disappointed to see there were no marks on their flanks.

"Congratulations!" smiled Twilight Sparkle, trotting up to the crusaders. "Job well done!"

"But we *still* don't have our cutie marks," said Sweetie Belle sadly. "Perhaps we were trying *too* hard?"

"We need to embrace our true talent . . . comedy!" shouted the young ponies, galloping off excitedly.

Twilight Sparkle shook her head and laughed. She knew that each pony would discover her true destiny and get her cutie mark . . . one day!

THE EQUESTRIA GAMES

START

The Equestria Games are being held in the Crystal Empire. Help your Ponyville friends succeed by making your way along the board. Let the games begin!

Find your six pony friends on the sticker sheet. Choose one to play with, then stick this onto card to make a counter. You'll also need a dice and at least one friend to play with. Throw the dice and then take it in turns to move around the board. The first one to reach the end is the winner!

1

2

14

15

13

Spike needs help to light the torch.
MISS A GO

16

Your team wins a silver medal!
MOVE FORWARD FOUR SPACES

17

18

You win a gold medal!
MOVE FORWARD FIVE SPACES

19

20

21

Uh oh! There's an ice arrow flying right at you.
MISS A GO

3

4

The train breaks down
on the way to the
Crystal Empire.

MISS A GO

5

6

7

The Crystal Empire ponies
carry you.

MOVE FORWARD
FIVE SPACES

8

10

You can't find the
Ponyville flag!

GO BACK
TWO SPACES

to look for it.

12

11

9

22

23

Bulk Biceps wins a bronze
medal in the weight lifting!

MOVE FORWARD
TWO SPACES

24

FINISH
25

You did it! Ponyville
has won more medals
than anyone else
in Equestria!

Hello, Sweetie Belle!

This young unicorn is the third member of the Cutie Mark Crusaders!

Rarity's relative: Sweetie Belle is Rarity's little sister.

Sweet singing: Sweetie Belle has a simply gorgeous singing voice. When she sings, even the birds and the butterflies stop to listen!

Did you know . . . As well as having a beautiful voice, Sweetie Belle also writes music *and* lyrics. She is one talented pony!

Pony personality: Although Sweetie Belle is the youngest of the Cutie Mark Crusaders, she always keeps up with Scootaloo and Apple Bloom.

A helping hoof: Sweetie Belle adores her big sis Rarity, and loves to help out in the Carousel Boutique. However, she is a little bit clumsy, and she sometimes ends up making a mess!

Cutie Mark Crusader Colouring Fun!

Use your favourite pens and pencils to colour in this picture of the three best friends. Don't forget to add stickers, too!

CUTIE MARK CRUSADERS

CUTIE MARK CRUSADERS

Your Perfect Pet Pal

Fluttershy adores *all* animals, and her special animal friend is Angel Bunny. Answer the questions below so this pet-mad pony can match you with your perfect pal!

How would you describe yourself?
- ⓐ Independent and relaxed
- ⓑ Sociable with lots of energy
- ⓒ Cuddly and bouncy!
- ⓓ Shy and kind

What's your favourite colour?
- ⓐ Ice blue
- ⓑ Warm orange
- ⓒ Grassy green
- ⓓ Snowy white

Mostly ⓐs

Your perfect pet is a cat like Opalescence!

You'd like a pet to hang out with who is happy to chill out alone when you're having fun with your other friends.

Mostly ⓑs

Your perfect pet is a dog like Winona!

You'd suit a loyal and energetic pet pal who can keep up with you.

If you could have a super-power, what would it be?

(a) You wish you could jump over the tallest building!

(b) To eat lots of delicious food without *ever* getting full!

(c) To run around all day without getting tired!

(d) You'd love to fly up into space!

What are you looking for in a pet?

(a) A fun but independent friend

(b) A loyal, lifelong companion

(c) Someone soft to cuddle!

(d) An unusual pet

What would your perfect day involve?

(a) A lovely lie-in, then a play date with friends

(b) A long walk in the park, followed by a swim

(c) Hanging out with pals in the countryside

(d) A quiet day, followed by a party in the evening!

Mostly (c)s

Your perfect pet is a bunny like Angel!

You're ideally suited to a cute, bouncy pet who likes cuddles (and carrots!)

Mostly (d)s

Your perfect pet is an owl like Owlowiscious!

This wise bird would suit your independent personality and quirky outlook on life.

37

BEWARE OF THE BADDIES!

Equestria is full of friendly ponies, but there are also some mean fiends to look out for . . .

NIGHTMARE MOON

Princess Luna, Princess Celestia's younger sister, became unhappy with looking after the night, and her bitterness transformed her into Nightmare Moon! One of the very first tasks for Twilight Sparkle and her friends was to find the Elements of Harmony and return Princess Luna to her true self.

DISCORD

This villainous creature is *very* tricksy! He uses his magic to cause chaos, and can make the very best of friends turn against each other. Discord has the head of a horse, the beard of a goat, the tail of a dragon *and* each of his arms and legs look different!

THE GREAT AND POWERFUL TRIXIE

Trixie is a travelling magician who causes trouble wherever she goes! Trixie is no more magical than other unicorns, but she likes to boast and show off about her powers.

Pesky Parasprites

These little critters may look cute, but they are a real munching menace! Able to multiply very quickly, these hungry creatures started to eat their way through Ponyville. Luckily, clever Pinkie Pie managed to lead the sprites away by playing many musical instruments. Phew!

Queen Chrysalis

This cross queen is a shape shifter, and she can make herself look like whoever she wants! This rogue royal did her best to ruin the wedding of Princess Cadance and Prince Shining Armour, but clever Twilight Sparkle saved the special day.

Gilda the Griffon

Gilda and Rainbow Dash were old pals from flying school, but when Gilda visited Ponyville, she was mean to *everyone*, especially Pinkie Pie! It wasn't long before Gilda showed everyone that she was a real 'mean meanie-pants'.

King Sombra

Spooky King Sombra has such great powers that he was able to take over the Crystal Empire, enslaving all the poor ponies who live there! He has a twisted grey unicorn horn and super-sharp fangs.

You're the Star!

Now it's your turn to star in your very own My Little Pony adventure. Fill in the blanks to create your own story!

It's a sunny day in Ponyville, and you and your friends Twilight Sparkle, Rainbow Dash, _____ and _____ are going to visit Pinkie Pie in the Sugarcube Corner Sweet Shoppe. But when you get there, you're horrified to see that all the _____ and _____ have disappeared, AND there's no sign of Pinkie Pie!

"Oh no!" you cry. "This can only be the work of _____! We must find our friend!"

You and _____ take to the skies to search for Pinkie Pie. You fly high above the clouds, but there's no sign of your friend.

You bump into Applejack, who says she has seen a trail of sweets and _____ leading to Canterlot!

You and all your pony friends fly up to Canterlot Castle. The trail leads you to the ballroom and there, alongside _____, is Pinkie Pie! She tells you that she's brought all of her _____ and _____ to Canterlot Castle to throw a special party for YOU to say thanks for being such an amazing friend!

You and your pony pals tuck into an amazing feast of your favourite foods, including _____ and _____ .

Then there's a display of incredible _____ up in the sky.

What a magical day it's been!

Turn to page 62 for the answers.

Use your stickers to add more snowflakes, presents and pretty garlands to the snowy scene!

Christmas Counting

It's Christmas time! The Cutie Mark Crusaders are helping Twilight Sparkle to get organised for the fun festivities. How many of the following can you spot?

Christmas trees

Stockings

Christmas presents

Snowflakes

Santa hats

41

Fabulous Fortune Teller

The ponies love to get crafty, and this fortune teller is one of their favourite things to make!

Once you have made the fortune teller, follow the 'how to play' instructions to enjoy your magical creation.

You will need:

✳ A square piece of plain paper

✳ Stickers

✳ Pens or pencils

1 Fold each corner of the piece of paper into the centre

2 When all four corners have been folded, your fortune teller should look like this:

3 Turn the paper over so the folded sides are face down.

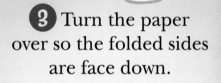

4 Fold over all the corners into the centre.

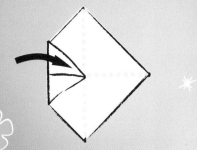

5 Next, write the numbers 1-8 on each of the triangles.

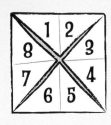

6 Hold the paper in front of you and fold it in half.

7 Now unfold and fold the piece of paper in half again, horizontally this time.

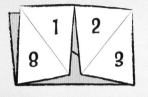

8 Open up each flap and write a fortune on each triangle. There will be eight in total. You can make up the fortunes, or see the list for suggestions!

9 Turn the fortune teller over, and use your stickers to add a different pony on each of the four outer flaps.

10 Flip the fortune teller over so that the numbers are face up. Fold the square in half and slip your thumb and pointing finger under the four flaps. Now you're ready to play!

Why not decorate your fortune teller with more pretty stickers?

How To Play

1 Ask a friend to pick one of the four ponies on the outside flaps.

2 Moving the flaps from side to side for each letter, spell out the name of the pony they have chosen.

3 Open the fortune teller to reveal the numbers and ask your friend to pick one. Count out the number they have chosen by moving the flaps in and out and side to side. Then ask them to pick another number and reveal the fortune you have written on the inside flap underneath this number.

Suggestions for Fortunes

You will make a new friend today!

It's going to be sunny soon

You will do a good deed today

You will travel somewhere new

Good fortune will be yours

Your hidden talents will soon be revealed

You will go to a sleepover soon

ARE YOU A **MY LITTLE PONY** SUPER FAN?

Why did Twilight Sparkle originally go to Ponyville?
- a To stay with relatives
- b She just fancied a change of scenery
- c To study the magic of friendship
- d To be Princess Celestia's representative

Which Element of Harmony does Rarity represent?
- a Kindness
- b Generosity
- c Laziness
- d Fun!

What is Applejack's grandmother called?
- a Granny Smith
- b Granny Pith
- c Grandma Green
- d Grandmother Crunch

What is the name of Pinkie Pie's pet alligator?
- a Toothy
- b Gummy
- c Sammy
- d Hungry

What is Spike's favourite food?

a Cherry pie
b Worms
c Gems
d Gold

How did Rainbow Dash get her cutie mark?

a She found it in the clouds
b It turned up after she baked a delicious cake
c It was given to her as a present
d It appeared after she performed a rare Sonic Rainboom

What is the name of the forest near where Fluttershy lives?

a Wandering Woods
b Faraway Forest
c Everfree Forest
d Evergreen Wood

What colour is Princess Celestia's mane?

a Rainbow-coloured
b Pink
c Red
d Black

How many did you get right?

8 out of 8: WOW, you really are a My Little Pony SUPER FAN! There's nothing you don't know about the ponies!

5–7: Great job, you know lots about your pony pals!

1–4: Good effort, but there's much more to find out!

None: Oh dear! But never mind – you're going to have lots of fun learning all about your My Little Pony friends.

Turn to page 62 for the answers.

It Ain't Easy Being Breezies

"Ok, everyone," said Fluttershy, smiling at her best friends. "The adorable creatures known as Breezies are coming through Ponyville *today*!"

Pinkie Pie jumped up and down with excitement as Rainbow Dash revealed that *she* was going to create the special breeze that would carry the little creatures back to their native land.

Fluttershy explained that Rainbow Dash's breeze would activate the Breezies' magic. This magic stopped the little creatures' special pollen from being blown away as they travelled to a magical portal that led them home. The portal was only open for two more days!

Later than day, as Ponyville prepared for the arrival of the Breezies, Rarity arrived looking super-shiny in a sequinned outfit!

When Fluttershy explained that the outfit might reflect the sun and shine in the eyes of the Breezies, knocking them off course, kind Rarity took off her sparkly jacket.

Then, as Twilight Sparkle practised her welcome speech, the ponies spotted something coming over the horizon. It was the Breezies!

As the adorable tiny winged ponies flew by, carrying their precious bags of pollen, disaster struck. A leaf blew straight through the group, splitting it in two! Rainbow Dash tried desperately to change the breeze so the two groups could rejoin, but it was too late!

Fluttershy spoke to the left-behind Breezies in their language. She needed to come up with a plan to help them on their way . . .

Fluttershy decided to take the Breezies home with her so that they could have a rest. The kind-hearted pony looked after them all, fetching food and water and keeping them warm.

"We need to go home right now!" cried Seabreeze, the leader of the Breezies. "It's *their* fault we got lost," he said crossly, pointing at the rest of the group. This tiny creature didn't seem to get on with the others at all!

But the other Breezies didn't want to leave. They were enjoying Fluttershy looking after them!

The next day, Rainbow Dash and her two pegasus helpers came to see if the Breezies were ready for a new breeze to take them home. But the little creatures were having *so* much fun with Fluttershy, they didn't want to leave!

Then Fluttershy noticed that Seabreeze had disappeared. She knew that the tiny Breezie would be in lots of trouble all alone out there in Ponyville, without the special breeze to carry him safely. And sure enough, when Fluttershy caught up with Seabreeze a few minutes later, he was about to be attacked by an angry hive of bees!

Fluttershy firmly told the mean bees to leave the Breezie alone. As Seabreeze explained he was just desperate to get home, Fluttershy realised that although she had enjoyed looking after her tiny new friends, it was time for them to be on their way.

Rushing back home with Seabreeze, Fluttershy told the group of Breezies firmly that it was time for them to leave. She felt awful being so stern with the little creatures, but it was the only way!

Rainbow Dash and her helpers tried hard to create the perfect breeze for the Breezies. But it was impossible to get it just right. The breeze was either too gentle or too strong!

"I have a spell that might help," said Twilight Sparkle. Concentrating hard, the pony friends were soon surrounded by magic – and then they all changed into teeny-tiny Breezies!

Then Rainbow Dash was able to create a breeze that was just the right strength to carry *all* the Breezies through the air.

Seabreeze was very kind to his fellow Breezies as they struggled to fly the long distance home. Finally, after a very long time, the tiny, tired Breezies reached the portal into their world. Fluttershy and her friends accompanied the creatures through the portal.

The Breezies were so pleased to see their family and friends! Fluttershy and the other ponies knew they had to go before the portal closed and they were stuck in the Breezies' world forever. Seabreeze gave Fluttershy a beautiful flower. "Something to remember us by, and thank you!" he said.

"My experience with the Breezies has taught me that kindness can take many forms, and sometimes being *too* kind isn't a good thing!" said Fluttershy, smiling at her pony friends as they zipped through the portal back into their own world.

Twilight Sparkle turned them back into ponies once more. And with that, the six friends started on their long journey home to Ponyville.

CAKE CHAOS

Pinkie Pie has been busy baking at the Sugarcube Corner, and now there are cakes EVERYWHERE! Can you guess who is hidden behind each pile of sweet treats?

Use your stickers to add even more cakes to the scene.

Funny Fillies!

Here are some of Pinkie Pie's favourite jokes!

Q: Why does Fluttershy speak so softly?

A: Because she's a little hoarse!

Q: What do you call a long-distance race held in Ponyville?

A: A mareathon!

Q: What flower is on your face?

A: Two-lips!

Why do we put candles on top of a birthday cake?

Because it's too difficult to put them on the bottom!

Q: What do you call a pony that lives next door?

A: A neigh-bour!

Which farm animal is always on time?

A watch dog!

Q: What did the rabbit say to the carrot?

A: It's been nice gnawing you!

Q: What do you call a pile of kittens?

A: a meowntain!

Tidy-Up Time

Oh no! Spike cast a spell to help
him tidy up the Golden Oak Library,
but it's gone wrong and made a terrible mess!
Can you help him clean up by finding all
the objects that shouldn't be in this scene?
Quick, before Twilight Sparkle
comes home!

Turn to page 62 for the answers.

53

Amazing Artist

Rarity is a super-talented artist, always sketching and drawing fabulous fashions in her boutique! Can you draw this pretty pony, following the instructions? It's a good idea to ask a grown-up to help you the first time.

Step 1
Using a pencil, draw a circle for the head and add a horizontal line through the centre. Directly below the head shape, draw an egg shape for the body. Now draw an arched line for the tail coming from this.

Step 2
Now it's time to create Rarity's beautiful face! Using a pen from this stage on, carefully draw her left cheek and the top line of the eyes. The line of the right eye should continue on to form her nose and chin.

Step 3
Draw Rarity's pointed ears. Now add a small dot for her nostril and a pretty smile!

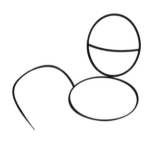

Step 4
Add the stripes for Rarity's unicorn horn, and then draw her large eyes. It's a good idea to practice drawing these a few times on a separate piece of paper! Add pupils and long lashes to the eyes.

Step 5

Now, using one continuous line, start the neck at the base of Rarity's head and curve this down to the body shape, forming her back, one hind leg and her stomach.

Step 6

Now add Rarity's second hind leg, and then draw in the two front legs.

Step 7

Now add Rarity's beautiful arched tail and her fabulous mane. You may need to practice these a few times on a separate piece of paper. Don't forget the small curl in her mane – remember, Rarity is always styled to perfection!

Step 8

Now add some detail to the mane and tail, as shown, and don't forget her three beautiful cutie marks! When you've finished doing this you can use a rubber to get rid of the pencil guides you drew at step 1.

Step 9

Well done!
Now use your best pens and pencils to colour in your picture.

Why not use your stickers to create a fabulous outfit for your fantastically fashionable friend?

Keeping Up With Rainbow Dash!

Rainbow Dash is always on the move, zooming around the skies of Equestria and keeping everything in order! This super-active pony knows how important it is to stay healthy. Here are her top tips for having fun and keeping fit.

Start the Day the Right Way

Rainbow Dash always eats a healthy breakfast of cereal, fruit and toast. Flying really builds up an appetite!

Super Scooting!

Rainbow Dash's friend Scootaloo uses her scooter to get *everywhere*! Scooting is a great form of exercise and it's also super FUN!

Brilliant Bouncing

Jumping on a trampoline is a tip-top way of using your muscles and improving your balance. Can you jump as high as Pinkie Pie?

Walk the Dog!

Applejack's animal friend, Winona, loves going for long walks around Sweet Apple Acres. If you don't have a dog, ask a friend who does if you can go for a stroll with them.

Skip, Hop!

Rainbow Dash loves to skip to warm up her legs and wing muscles before a big flight! Pick up a skipping rope and see how many skips you can do in a minute.

Grab a Ball

There are so many games you can play with a ball, from tennis to football and catch to bowling! Always take a ball with you when you head out with friends.

Wonderful Water

It's very important to drink water to stay hydrated and healthy. Try to carry a bottle with you when you're out and about!

What's Your Sport?

All the ponies have their favourite activity and it's important to find a sport that suits you! Why not ask your mum or dad if you can try a new sport? You might find a sport you LOVE!

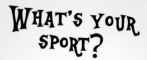

A Very Special Message

The My Little Ponies have told Princess Celestia what an amazing friend you are. She has a special message just for you, but to read it you need to unscramble her magic code! Use the grid below to work out what the message is.

BLF ZIV MLD ZM SLMLFIZIB NB ORGGOV KLMB!

A B C D E F G H I J K L M N O P Q R S T U V W X Y Z
Z Y X W V U T S R Q P O N M L K J I H G F E D C B A

_ _ _ _ _ _ _ _ _ _ _ _ _ _ _ _ _ _ _ _

_ _ _ _ _ _ _ _ _ _ _ _ _ _ _ _ _ _ _ _

Hairstyle Heaven

Each of the ponies has a unique mane and tail style. Here are some styling tips from your pony friends!

Twilight's Funky Fringe

Princess Twilight Sparkle has a super-sharp fringe, but there's no need to cut your hair to create a similar look! Follow these instructions to create a stylish side fringe.

1. Brush your hair, and then, using your hands, make a parting slightly to the left or right of the centre of your head, using a front section of hair.

2. Keeping hold of this hair, run your fingers through it and pull it to the front side of your head, towards your ear.

3. Twist the hair slightly and then use a hairgrip to pin your side fringe to your head. Arrange the rest of your hair to cover the hairgrip.

Lovely Loose Curls

Fluttershy's mane and tail has a natural wave, but even if your hair is very straight, you can easily create wonderful waves! This style works best with medium to long hair.

1. Before you go to bed, wash your hair and rub with a towel until it is nearly dry.

2. Separate your hair into sections, and then pin these up into a bun. The smaller the sections, the tighter the waves will be. Secure all the sections with a hairband and go to bed!

3. In the morning, unpin your hair and your waves will be revealed

Awesome Accessories!

There's nothing like a super-cool hair accessory to lift your look. Here's how some of the ponies wear theirs!

Apple Bloom's vibrant red hair bow keeps her mane out of her eyes!

Princess Celestia's stunning crown shows everyone she's the ruler of Equestria! A tiara or crown is a great accessory for humans, too.

Head for a hat! Mr Carrot Cake looks very smart in his peaked cap. Wearing a hat is a great way of standing out from the crowd, and it's fun to find a hat style that suits you!

Crossword Time

Test your knowledge of your pony friends with this cool crossword!

Across

1. Which pony has the sweetest tooth?
5. What is the name of Fluttershy's pet sidekick?
7. What is the name of Rainbow Dash's speedy heroes?
9. Which Cutie Mark Crusader rides a scooter?
10. The second name of Applejack's big brother

Down

2. What colour is Rarity's mane?
3. What type of pony is Rainbow Dash?
4. What is Princess Celestia's cutie mark?
6. Which empire does Princess Cadance rule?
8. Twilight Sparkle loves to read these!

Turn to page 62 for the answers.

FAREWELL, FRIENDS!

The ponies hope you've enjoyed their special annual – they've *really* enjoyed spending time with you! Here are their top tips for being a brilliant friend and having fun.

(F) Friends and family are the most important people in the world!

(A) Always stay true to what you believe in

(R) Respect and care for the world around you

(E) Eat well and be active!

(W) Wear clothes and accessories that are comfortable

(E) Enjoy your own company. It's good to have some down time!

(L) Laugh as much as possible!

(L) Learn new skills and embrace new experiences

Answers

Scootaloo's Speedy Word Search

Spot the Difference

Race to the Wonderbolts

Missing Marks

Christmas Counting

DID YOU FIND THE FOLLOWING?

Three Christmas trees
Six stockings
Eight presents
Four Santa hats
Ten snowflakes

Too Many Pinkie Pies

There are 16 Pinkie Pies
in the picture

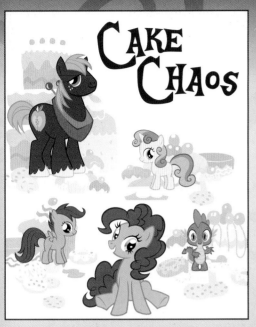

CAKE CHAOS

ARE YOU AN MLP SUPER FAN?

1. C – Twilight Sparkle came to Ponyville to study the magic of friendship
2. B – Rarity represents the element of Generosity
3. B – Pinkie Pie's pet alligator is called Gummy
4. D – Rainbow Dash got her cutie mark after she performed a Sonic Rainboom
5. C – Fluttershy lives near Everfree Forest
6. A – Applejack's grandmother is called Granny Smith
7. C – Spike's favorite food is gems
8. A – Princess Celestia has a beautiful rainbow-coloured mane

TIDY-UP TIME!

A Very Special Message

The special message
from Princess Celestia is:

YOU ARE
NOW AN
HONORARY
MY LITTLE
PONY!

Crossword Time

ACROSS

1. Which pony has the sweetest tooth?
PINKIE PIE

5. What is the name of Fluttershy's pet sidekick?
ANGEL

7. What is the name of Rainbow Dash's speedy heroes?
WONDERBOLTS

9. Which Cutie Mark Crusader rides a scooter?
SCOOTALOO

10. The second name of Applejack's big brother
MCINTOSH

DOWN

2. What colour is Rarity's mane?
PURPLE

3. What type of pony is Rainbow Dash?
PEGASUS

4. What is Princess Celestia's cutie mark?
SUN

6. Which empire does Princess Cadance rule?
CRYSTAL

8. Twilight Sparkle loves to read these!
BOOKS

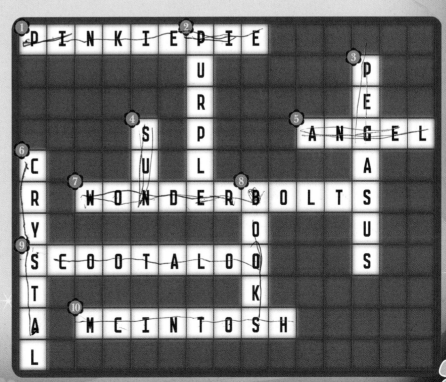

EXPLORE THE MAGICAL WORLD OF MY LITTLE PONY!

Orchard books are available from all good bookshops.
They can be ordered via our website: www.orchardbooks.co.uk,
or by telephone: 01235 827 702, or fax: 01235 827 703

ORCHARD